Watch me bloom when I learn to wait

A coping story for children about waiting,
how to practice patience and adapt to unexpected delays

Written by Grace Ledden, MA, BCBA
Illustrated by CyAn Platas

Paperback edition   ISBN: 978-1-962410-24-3
Digital edition   ISBN: 978-1-962410-25-0

Published by Daily Bloom LLC - Tennessee, USA

www.mydailybloom.com

To all the families who walk the unique path of autism.

This book is dedicated to you, in recognition of the journey you embark on every day. May it serve as a small reminder that you are seen, you are loved, and you are not alone. Here's to the extraordinary lives that you lead, and the stories you continue to write every day.

This book belongs to

_____

Hello there, my name is Maya. I love the color pink, dancing, and drawing pictures.

Today is my birthday and I am five years old! I am so excited to have a birthday party! My party is going to be pink with unicorns and pink cupcakes. All of my friends and family are going to come.

But the hardest part about turning five has been having to wait!

Waiting is hard for me. You see, I have autism and sometimes I get really upset when I have to wait for things.

Before my birthday, whenever I looked at the calendar, the countdown to my birthday party seemed to crawl by so slowly. Each morning, I would wake up wondering, "Is it my birthday yet?" But each time, the answer was, "Not yet, Maya. We still have to wait a bit longer."

Last Saturday was the hardest morning. I felt like a race car stuck at the starting line, ready to zoom but stuck waiting for the green light. I was getting mad and frustrated waiting for my birthday. It was taking too long. Why couldn't I be five yet?

Just as I was starting to have big feelings, I saw a burst of sparkles appear at the bottom of my bed. A pretty gnome with long curly hair and a white hat appeared.

Where did she come from? I had never seen her before!

"Hello, Maya. My name is Jasmine, and I am your Bloom Buddy!" she said. "I see that you have big feelings right now as you wait for your birthday. Waiting can be hard, but it can also be fun if you try."

"How can waiting be fun?" I asked with surprise.

Jasmine handed me a long, colorful paper chain with pink links in it. "You know, Maya," she said. "Whenever I have to wait for something special, I make a colorful paper chain with as many links as days that I have to wait. Each day, you can remove one link in the chain. As the chain gets shorter, your birthday gets closer!"

"That does sound like fun," I said to Jasmine as I played with the pink links on the chain. "I'm very good at counting. I counted 7 links in the chain. That means it is 7 days until my birthday!"

"It sure does," Jasmine replied.

"You know, Maya, some days are going to be harder than others, but that's okay! On those days, it's a good idea to do a creative activity for your birthday to turn your wiggly jiggly jitters into something fun."

"Maybe I could plan games for my party? Or I could make party favors for my friends!", I said excitedly.

"Those are great ideas, Maya! Remember, it's okay to feel upset when you have to wait. If you ever need me again, think of me, and I will be here to help you."

With that, Jasmine did a little twirl and disappeared in a shower of shimmering sparkles.

Every morning when I woke up, I would take off one link from the chain, and then spend time drawing plans for my party.

Before I knew it, the paper chain was much shorter, and my birthday was just around the corner.

Yesterday there was just one chain link left. Mommy and I decided to bake my favorite pink sprinkle cupcakes for the party. We mixed the ingredients together, scooped the batter into the cupcake molds and put them in the oven to bake.

"Maya, you've been such a wonderful helper," Mommy smiled. "Now, we need to set the timer. Baking requires a bit of waiting."

Waiting again? Waiting is always hard, but it seemed so much harder when the cupcakes smelled so yummy. I tapped my foot impatiently, peeking at the oven every few seconds, waiting for the timer to beep. The oven timer was taking so long.

Finally, the cupcakes were ready!

"Can we decorate them now?" I asked Mommy.

"Not yet, Maya. We have to let the cupcakes cool down first before we can decorate them," she said.

I had already waited so long for the cupcakes to come out of the oven and couldn't wait any longer. I was getting the wiggly jiggly jitters and started to stomp my feet and clench my fists. My face felt like it was getting hotter than the oven.

Just as I was about to have big feelings, I felt a tap on my shoulder.

Jasmine was in our kitchen!

"Hey there, birthday girl," Jasmine grins. "Maya, I can see that you're finding it hard to wait for the cupcakes to cool. I also find it hard to wait sometimes when it comes to yummy food."

"Really?" I asked as I flapped my hands.

"Yes, but when I am waiting, I set a timer and then find something fun to do while the timer is counting down. You can do this too. You can ask Mommy to set a timer for you so that you know when the cupcakes are cool enough to decorate. Do you want to try this now?" Jasmine asked.

I turned to Mommy and asked, "Mommy, can you set a timer for me to tell me when the cupcakes will be ready to decorate?"

"Sure, Maya. I will set a timer for fifteen minutes."

Jasmine continued, "While we wait for the cupcakes to cool, how about we draw some cupcake decorating ideas? Let's channel that energy into something creative!"

With Jasmine's encouragement, I started to draw my ideas. I drew cupcakes with pink stars and red hearts and cupcakes with the letter "M" for Maya on them. All of my cupcakes were covered in pink sprinkles.

Just then the timer beeped. The cupcakes were cool enough to decorate. The waiting had gone by really fast! I was so excited to finally start decorating the cupcakes!

"Well done, Maya. Your drawings are wonderful! Your cupcakes will look beautiful and delicious," Jasmine said.

I was so happy that Jasmine helped my wiggly jiggly jitters become little feelings.

"Remember, it's okay to feel upset when you have to wait. If you ever need me again, think of me, and I will be here to help you," Jasmine said.

With a little twirl, Jasmine disappeared once more in a shower of shimmering sparkles.

My paper chain is all gone!
This means today is my birthday and the day of my party!

My tummy feels like it is full of butterflies fluttering with excitement. The garden is decorated with unicorns, pink balloons, and the cupcakes I helped make and decorate are laid out. But I have to wait again, this time for my friends to arrive!

It's two o'clock, the official start of the party, but none of my friends are here yet. Five minutes pass, then ten, then fifteen minutes. With each passing minute, I get more wiggly and more jiggly. I feel like a balloon that is getting bigger and bigger and is about to burst.

Just as I am about to have big feelings, I remember what Jasmine said to me. I can make waiting fun and do an activity while I wait.
"Mommy!" I call. "Can you put on my favorite music, please?"
"Of course, sweetheart!"

Soon, I hear my favorite song, and I start to dance and twirl in the garden. After dancing for a short while, I feel my big feelings start to go away like a balloon slowly deflating. My big feelings have become little feelings, and I start smiling and laughing. I had forgotten that I was waiting for my friends to arrive.

Just then, I hear a sound. I turn around to see my friend Priya at the gate and right behind her is Olivia and Sofia. A few minutes later, my other friends Jalen, Noah, Veer, and Gabriel arrive.

Suddenly, Jasmine appears. "Well done, Maya," she says. "You were very good at waiting and did an activity while you waited for your friends to arrive. You danced and twirled while waiting to pass the time. See, waiting can be fun!"

I smile and clap my hands. My favorite music is still playing but now all of my friends are here.

"I'm so proud of you, Maya. Sometimes things don't happen exactly when we want them to, but that doesn't mean they won't happen at all."

"Thank you for teaching me how to wait," I say as I smile at Jasmine. "Remember, any time you need help with waiting just think of me and I'll be by your side to help! I'll see you on our next adventure. Happy Birthday, Maya!"

Jasmine taught me that waiting can be hard and that's okay! Waiting can be so much fun and is always worth the wait!
And with a little twirl, Jasmine disappeared once more into a shower of shimmering sparkles, and I celebrated my birthday with my friends.

Watch Your Child Bloom with More Daily Bloom Coping Stories!

www.mydailybloom.com

Help Me Grow - Share Your Feedback!

As an independent author, your review makes a big difference. It helps me reach new readers and continue creating stories that enrich little ones' lives.

Please scan the QR code below to leave a review and discover more from Daily Bloom.

As a thank you, you can also download exclusive content featuring the Bloom Buddies!

PRIVACY.FLOWCODE.COM

About the Author

Grace Ledden, MA, BCBA, is a Board Certified Behavior Analyst specializing in creating individualized support and treatment for young children diagnosed with autism and their families. Grace graduated with a Master's degree in Applied Behavior Analysis with an emphasis in autism. Grace seeks to create visual supports and tools that will help young children and their families navigate their world and lead a more meaningful life. Grace strives to be part of creating a world that is more inclusive, accepting, and understanding of neurodiversity.

Thank you for choosing to share Watch Me Bloom When I Learn to Wait with your child.

This addition to our series aims to address another aspect of children's emotional lives— the art of waiting. I wanted to offer our young readers not just a reflection of their own feelings of impatience or anticipation, but also a guide on how to turn those feelings into an opportunity for creativity and growth.

This story is inspired by the unique experiences and challenges that I've seen many children with autism often face. With Jasmine appearing during Maya's moments of anticipation and frustration, Maya learns the valuable skill of patience and discovers the fun that can be had—even when waiting for something as exciting as a birthday.

Like a bud patiently waiting to bloom, children too will flourish when they learn how to handle life's pauses and delays. Let's empower them with the emotional tools they'll need for a lifetime of growth and happiness.

- Grace Ledden

More ways to bloom
when learning to wait

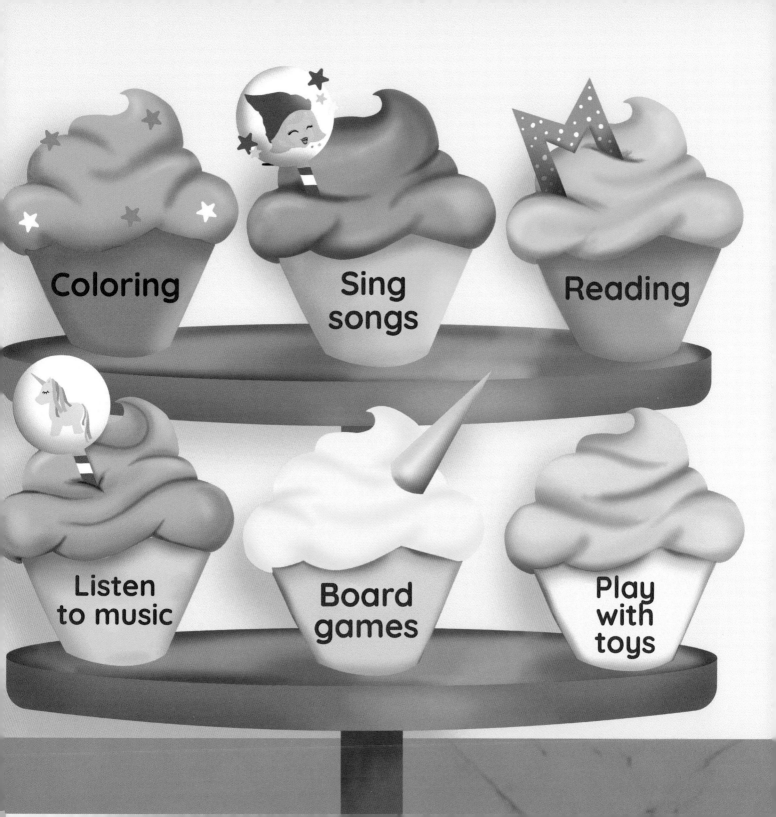

Coloring

Sing songs

Reading

Listen to music

Board games

Play with toys

Printed in Great Britain
by Amazon

44693987R00027